HERMAN'S HERE!

And he brought his friends—the guy who told you how the movie ended . . . the cook with only one recipe (leftovers) . . . even the grocery cart with the crooked wheel—in an all-new collection of cartoon capers, starring the most lovable loser around! HERMAN is syndicated in more than 300 newspapers worldwide and is the creation of Jim Unger, who keeps coming up with fresh ways to look on the lighter side of life.

HERMAN

"Now what are you up to, Herman?"

by

JIM UNGER

A SIGNET BOOK

NEW AMERICAN LIBRARY

NAL BOOKS ARE AVAILABLE AT QUANTITY DISCOUNTS WHEN USED TO PROMOTE PRODUCTS OR SERVICES. FOR INFORMATION PLEASE WRITE TO PREMIUM MARKETING DIVISION. NEW AMERICAN LIBRARY. 1633 BROADWAY. NEW YORK. NEW YORK 10019.

Published by arrangement with Andrews, McMeel & Parker

The cartoons in "*Now What Are You Up To Herman?*" appeared originally in *The 1st Treasury of Herman.*

"Herman" is syndicated internationally by Universal Press Syndicate

SIGNET TRADEMARK REG U S PAT OFF AND FOREIGN COUNTRIES
REGISTERED TRADEMARK— MARCA REGISTRADA
HECHO EN CHICAGO. U S A

SIGNET, SIGNET CLASSIC, MENTOR, PLUME, MERIDIAN AND NAL BOOKS are published by New American Library, 1633 Broadway, New York, New York 10019

First Signet Printing, September, 1985

3 4 5 6 7 8 9 10 11

PRINTED IN THE UNITED STATES OF AMERICA

"Where do you think you get off taking out your own appendix?"

"Do you believe the nerve
of that guy whistling at
us like that?"

"He painted this one when he was 3 years old."

"D'you know 'Shine on Harvest Moon'?"

"Two million years ago, it ate nothing but caterpillars."

"Yeah, well as far as I'm concerned, bug killer is bug killer and you guys owe me a new screen door."

"I'll never forget the time you strapped me for talking in class."

"Can you send an ambulance to 27 Sycamore Drive in about six minutes?"

"You the guy who ordered the 'Grand Slam' pizza?"

"I hope it's not inconvenient. We're your new neighbors."

"Had enough music?"

"Allow me to introduce myself...I'm a basketball talent scout."

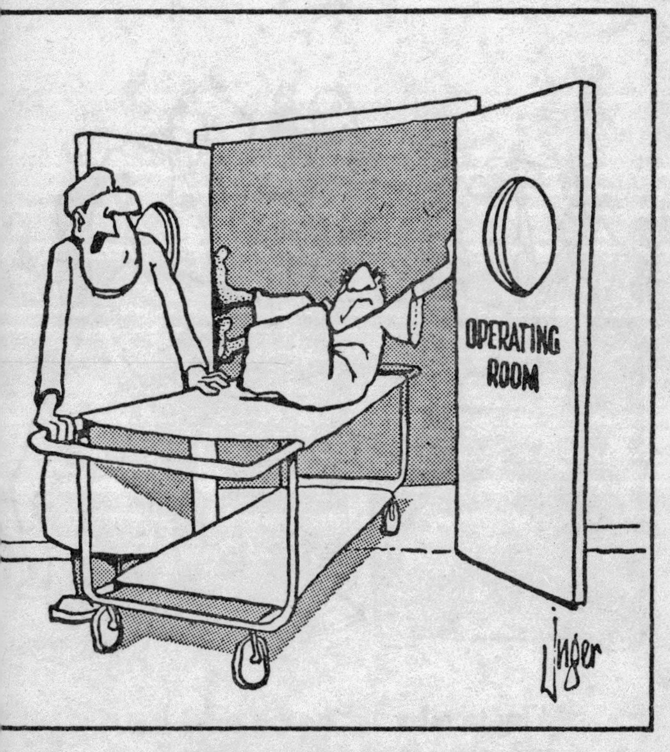

Er, Doc...can he have a quick look at your diploma?"

"Try to relax . . . he can smell fear."

"I know it's your first day, but you've got to accept the fact that some customers are just 'lookers'."

"You wouldn't believe how tough it is to get him up in the morning."

"Why don't you wear long socks 'til he learns to tell the difference?"

"You've got Egyptian flu. You're going to be a 'mummy.'"

"Don't sit on the bean-bag chair...it's got a split in it."

"Just you start something. My husband's a karate expert."

"Five bucks if you start practicing your violin."

"If you keep bugging me about getting married, I'm gonna break off our engagement."

"Hope you sent Johnny Carson the bill for the lumber."

"You'd never get to the moon. You'd need two hundred of those things."

"If you took my advice you'd throw away those bathroom scales. You're letting this weight-loss thing become an obsession."

"What happened! Did I touch a nerve?"

"You've DEFINITELY got the flu."

"I'm the baby-sitter. Where's the fridge?"

"My, my...you're the image of your father!"

"How come I have to pay the same air fare as a great lump like him?"

"What'sa matter with you...doncha like spaghetti?"

"The jury has found you not guilty, but I'm going to give you 2 years just to be on the safe side."

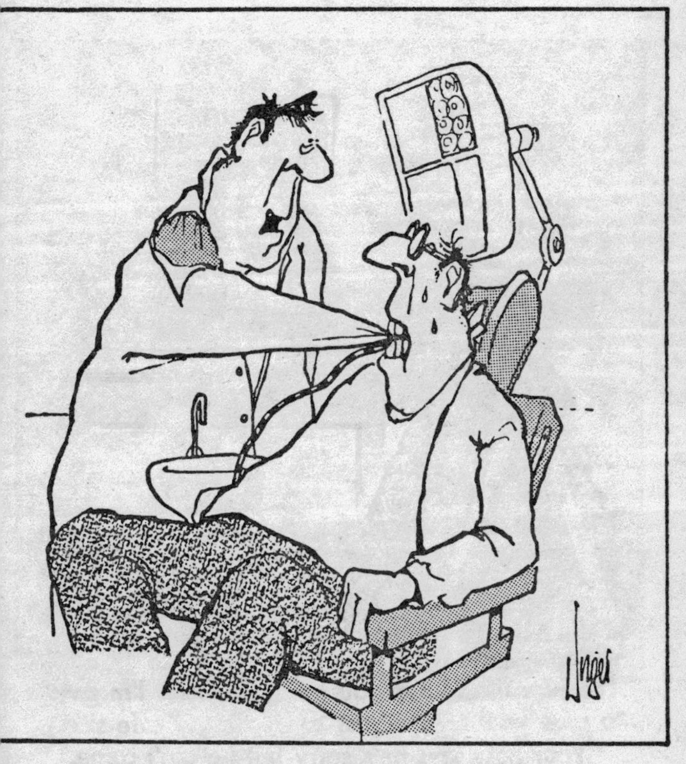

"I promise no more drilling if you let go."

"Your boss says he's sorry but he can't come."

"Chicken for breakfast, chicken for lunch, chicken for dinner. What d'you expect?"

"Oh, it's you! I thought it was a burglar."

"I can always tell when they're wearing 'elevator shoes.'"

"Are you eating properly and getting plenty of exercise?"

"The cat had a fit!"

"Are you going to drink this coffee or shall I throw it away?"

"SLOW DOWN...WATCH THAT PUSSY CAT...
TURN RIGHT HERE."

"I can't remember the last time you put your arm around me at the movies."

"Why don't you start going to bed earlier?"

"Get out! I haven't forgotten I fired you this morning."

"STAY!"

"Let's face it; if you'd really loved me, you'd have married someone else!"

"Will ya take a check?"

DO NOT
FEED
ALLIGATOR

"Who's calling? D'you know what time it is?"

"For the tenth time, I'm NOT going bowling."

"You're my last hope, Harry. Can I borrow your dinner jacket?"

"This is my first day. Do we get paid?"

"Leave the car keys just in case something grabs you out there."

"You've got to start sometime. Why don't you operate on this one?"

"I knew you hadn't quit!"

"Hang on to your tickets! You may have trouble bringing that kid out."

"I said 'I wanna marry your daughter when I get some money' and he gave me twenty bucks."

"Did you know your front wheel fell off?"

"GET OFF THAT OILY MAN WITH YOUR BEST SHOES ON."

"Happy birthday...I dropped your cake."

"LADIES AND GENTLEMEN, the bride and groom!"

"Listen...if we get this right, we'll be famous."

"I told him he needed more feathers."

"Of course you don't lose YOUR ball...you never hit it more than six feet."

"Sorry to keep you both waiting out here. Where's your wife?"

"Six months at Art College and you say 'What's it s'posed to be?'"

"Watch out for his screw-ball."

"If you let it go maybe it'll stop screaming."

"So that's your story—you hate to be late!"

"Don't spill this; it's goldfish."

"Size what?"

"I think I'll sell all my jewelry. I need the five dollars."

"For crying out loud! If it's that important to you, take the afternoon off."

"Is that everything, just a bar of soap?"

"First things first. Get your stomach off my desk."

"Okay, you've got five minutes to capture my interest."

"Did you feel the earthquake?"

"Hey, GET OFF MY LAND!"

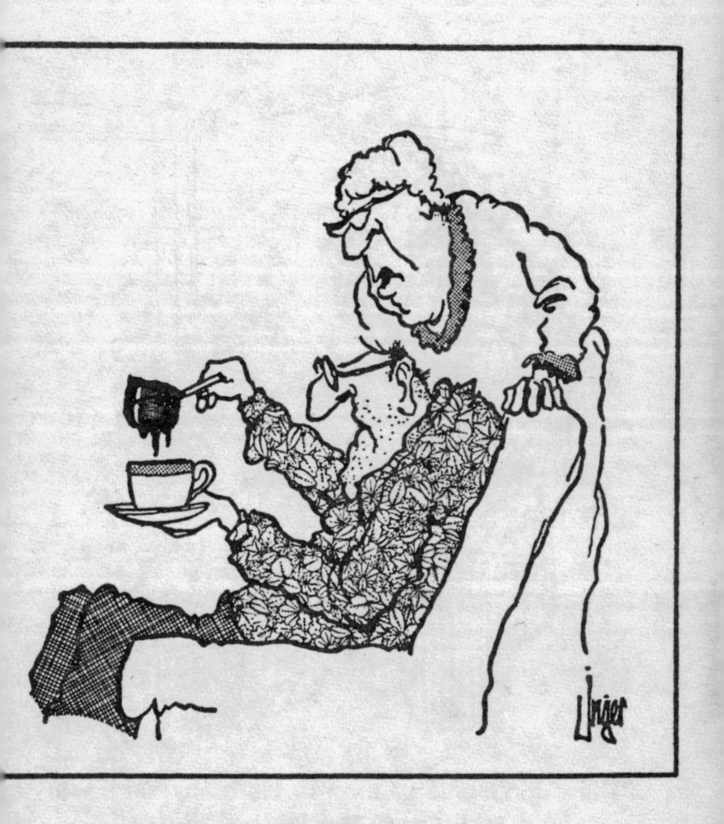

"You always said you liked it strong."

"They don't give us time to learn anything; we have to listen to the teacher all day."

"Another good feature of this home is that it's within a stone's throw of several schools."

"One seat at the front and one at the back."

"Well, well, my secret file tells me that since 1948 this is your grandmother's seventh funeral."

"Stop whining. I caught it so I'll carry it."

COOKING
MECHANICS

"Will you shove off. I'm sick of your jealousy!"

"Boy! . . . you sure know how to break a vow of silence."

"As your Latin professor, I can't say you've exactly made my day."

"Forget it. I'm never gonna get THAT hungry."

"That's fine!"

"I see you're taking a trip."

ABOUT THE AUTHOR

JIM UNGER was born in London, England. After surviving the blitz bombings of World War II and two years in the British Army, followed by a short career as a London bobby and a driving instructor, he immigrated to Canada in 1968, where he became a newspaper graphic artist and editorial cartoonist. For three years running he won the Ontario Weekly Newspaper Association's "Cartoonist of the Year" award. In 1974 he began drawing HERMAN for Universal Press Syndicate, with instant popularity. HERMAN is now enjoyed by 60 million daily and Sunday newspaper readers all around the world. His cartoon collections, THE HERMAN TREASURIES, became paperback bestsellers.

Jim Unger now lives in Nassau, Bahamas.